BUNNY CAKES

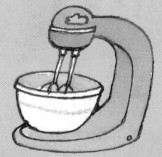

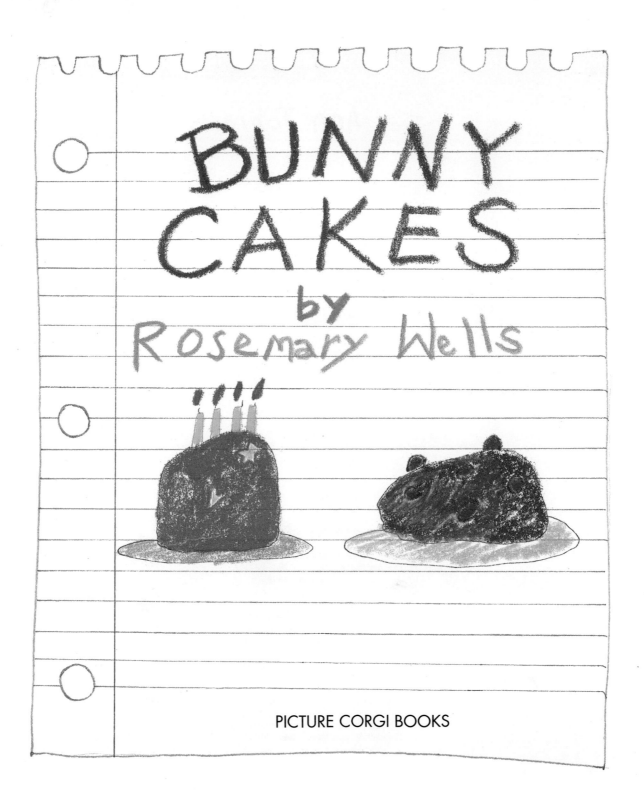

BUNNY CAKES

by
Rosemary Wells

PICTURE CORGI BOOKS

For Ann Tobias

A PICTURE CORGI BOOK: 0 552 545821

First published in the USA in 1997 by Dial Books
for Young Readers

First published in Great Britain by Doubleday, a division of
Transworld Publishers Ltd

PRINTING HISTORY
Doubleday edition published 1997
Picture Corgi edition published 1998

Picture Corgi Books are published by Transworld Publishers Ltd.
61 - 63 Uxbridge Road, Ealing, London W5 5SA,
in Australia by Transworld Publishers (Australia) Pty. Ltd,
15 - 25 Helles Avenue, Moorebank, NSW 2170,
and in New Zealand by Transworld Publishers (NZ) Ltd,
3 William Pickering Drive, Albany, Auckland.

Printed in Belgium by Proost Book Productions

It was Grandma's birthday.

Max made her an earthworm birthday cake.

"No, Max," said Max's sister, Ruby. "We are going to make

Grandma an angel surprise cake with raspberry-fluff icing."

Max wanted to help.

"Don't touch anything, Max," said Ruby.

But it was too late.
Ruby sent Max to the shop
with a list that said:

EGGS

Max wanted Red-Hot Marshmallow Squirters for his earthworm
cake. So he wrote "Red-Hot Marshmallow Squirters" on his list.

The shop-keeper, Mr Barley, could not read Max's writing.
"Eggs!" said Mr Barley, and he gave Max eggs.

Max brought the eggs home to Ruby.

"Don't bump the table, Max!" said Ruby.

But it was too late.
Ruby sent Max back to the
shop with a list that said:

This time Max wrote "Red-Hot Marshmallow Squirters"
in a different way.

Max hoped and hoped for his Squirters,
but Mr Barley still couldn't read Max's writing.
"Milk!" said Mr Barley, and he gave Max milk.

Max brought the milk home to Ruby.

"There's a yellow line on the floor, Max," said Ruby.

"You can't step over that line."

But Max crossed the line anyway.

Over went the flour.

Ruby got out her pencil.

This time Max wrote "Red-Hot Marshmallow Squirters"
in the most beautiful writing he knew.

Max could almost taste the Marshmallow Squirters.

"Flour," said Mr Barley, and he gave Max flour.

When Max got home, there was
a sign on the kitchen door.
"Max, the kitchen is no place
for you," said Ruby.

Ruby finished making her cake.

She baked it and cooled it and iced it with
raspberry-fluff icing.
"It needs something else, Max," said Ruby.

"Birthday candles, silver stars, sugar hearts,
buttercream roses," wrote Ruby.
Meanwhile Max had a brand-new idea.

BIRTHDAY CANDLES
SILVER STARS
SUGAR HEARTS
BUTTERCREAM
ROSES

He drew a picture of Red-Hot
Marshmallow Squirters on Ruby's
list and ran to the shop.
He could not wait.

"Birthday candles, silver stars, sugar hearts,
buttercream roses!" said Mr Barley. "What's this?
Why, it must be Red-Hot Marshmallow Squirters!"

Ruby's cake looked just beautiful.

Max went out and put caterpillar icing on his earthworm cake.

Grandma was so thrilled, she didn't know which cake to eat first.